Daddy's Star
By: Freya Lavender Page

Foreword

Losing a loved one is very difficult, especially for children. It's important to talk to your child about their feelings and to provide a safe and supportive environment for them to grieve. Show them that their emotions are valid and important.

While you are reading the book, feel free to replace the words "Mommy" and "Daddy" with whomever is reading the story and whomever the child may have lost, or whomever is appropriate. Maybe Grandma/Grandpa was at the hospital or the child may want to talk to an ⎯⎯⎯/Uncle.

Whether or not you decide to change the story, I hope this book can be helpful. After reading the book, maybe you and the child can look up to the sky and pick out a star to help bring remembrance and comfort.

Remember that everyone grieves differently, and there's no right or wrong way to cope with loss. Patience, empathy, and understanding are key when helping a child navigate through the difficult process of grief and loss.

At the back of the book I have listed some advice for anyone trying to help a child who has lost someone they love.

Daddy's Star

Helping Children Cope with the Loss and Death of a Loved One Through Love and Remembrance

By: Freya Lavender Page

... have tickle-fights ...

... read books ...

... and look up at the stars.

One day, Emma's daddy got very sick,
and he had to go to the hospital.

Emma waited and waited for Daddy to come back, but he never did.

Her mommy told her that daddy had died. Emma felt sad and confused and started to cry. She didn't understand why her daddy was gone.

Her mommy listened to her when she talked about how she was feeling, and told her it was okay to cry and to feel sad, and that she was there for her.

Emma's mommy explained to her that sometimes when people get very old or very sick, their bodies stop working and they pass away.

Her mommy put her arm around her
and then said:

"The energy and love in a person's heart
does not go away when they die. Instead,
it flows all around us like a BIG HUG!"

That night, Emma noticed a bright star in the sky that reminded her of her daddy.

She decided to talk to the star ...

... and it made her feel like her
daddy was still with her.

Doing normal activities also helped Emma to feel better even though it was tough and she still felt sad.

Emma talked to her classmates about her daddy and how she was feeling. They were very kind and caring, and made her feel less alone.

Emma realized that even though her daddy was gone, she could still remember his love.

She looked at pictures of him and remembered all the fun times they had together.

Talking to Daddy's star made her feel better. The star reminded her that it's okay to be sad sometimes, and that it's important to talk about your feelings.

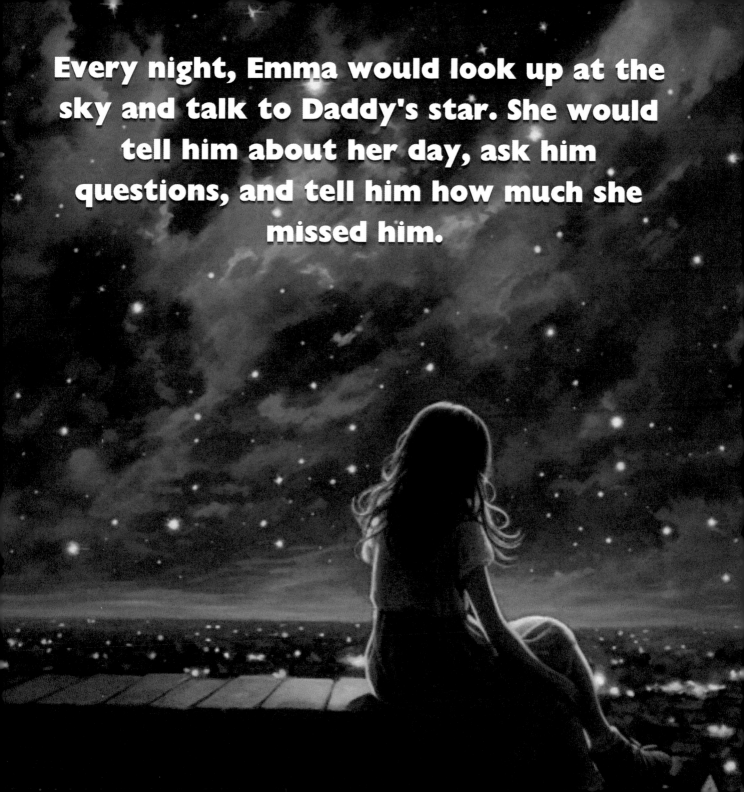

Every night, Emma would look up at the sky and talk to Daddy's star. She would tell him about her day, ask him questions, and tell him how much she missed him.

Emma knew that she would always miss her daddy, but she also knew that he was watching over her. She looked up at the stars, then closed her eyes and smiled, knowing that her daddy would always be with her.

The End

Afterword

Things to keep in mind when trying to help a child who has lost someone they love:

1. <u>Maintain routines and provide stability</u>. Help the child establish a sense of normalcy by maintaining their daily routines as much as possible. Consistency and stability can provide comfort during times of loss and change.
2. <u>Be available and present</u>. Let the child know that you are there for them and available to listen whenever they need to talk or express their feelings.
3. <u>Create an open and safe environment</u>, where the child feels safe to share their thoughts and emotions without judgment. Encourage them to express their feelings and provide reassurance that it's okay to feel sad, angry, or confused.
4. <u>Be a compassionate and attentive listener</u>. Give the child your full attention when they want to talk, and avoid dismissing or minimizing their emotions. Let them know that you care about what they have to say.
5. <u>Provide age-appropriate explanations</u>. Use simple and age-appropriate language to explain the concept of death and any related circumstances. Avoid euphemisms or complex explanations that may confuse them.
6. <u>Answer honestly</u>. Be honest and straightforward when answering questions about death. Use clear and concrete examples to help them understand, and be prepared for follow-up questions as their understanding evolves.
7. <u>Encourage expression through different outlets</u>. Encourage them to explore their emotions in a way that feels comfortable for them. Provide the child with various outlets to express their grief, like drawing, writing, or physical activities.
8. <u>If needed, seek additional support</u>. If the child continues to struggle with their grief, consider seeking additional support from professionals such as therapists or grief counselors who specialize in working with children.

Remember, each child grieves differently, so adjust based on their needs.

Made in the USA
Coppell, TX
29 August 2024

36616865R00017